BETTER THAN TV

SARA SWAN MILLER

Illustrated by Michael Chesworth

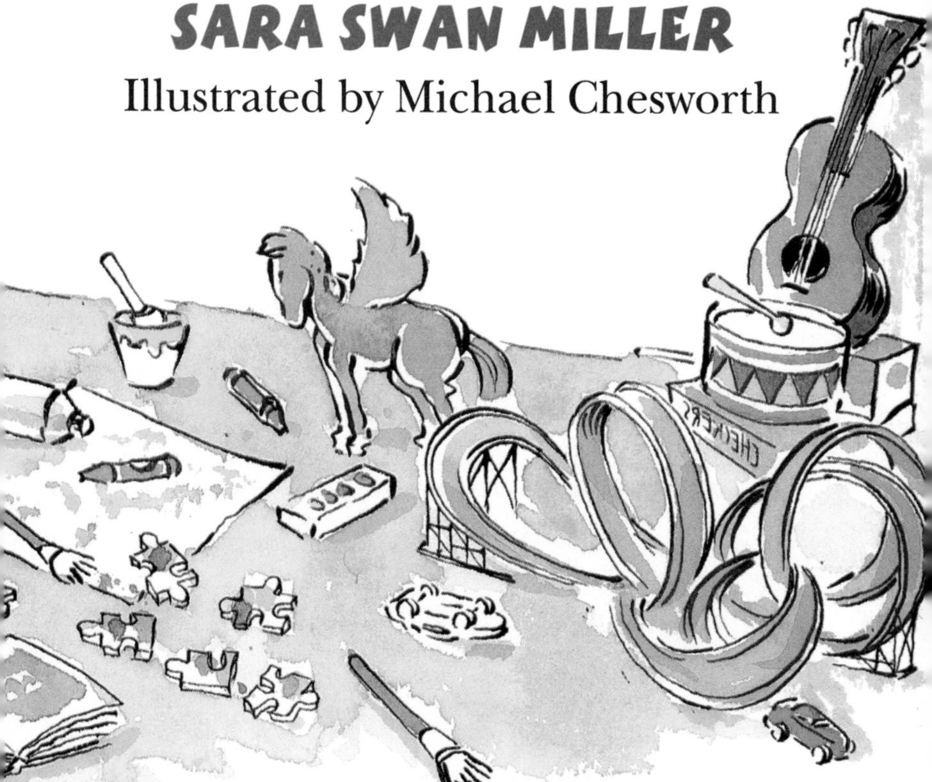
CHECKERS

A Yearling First Choice Chapter Book

For Chris and Erin—S.S.M.

Published by
Bantam Doubleday Dell Publishing Group, Inc.
1540 Broadway
New York, New York 10036

Text copyright © 1998 by Sara Swan Miller
Illustrations copyright © 1998 by Michael Chesworth
All rights reserved.

If you purchased a paperback edition of this book without a cover you should be aware that this book is stolen property. It was reported as "unsold and destroyed" to the publisher and neither the author nor the publisher has received any payment for this "stripped book."

Library of Congress Cataloging-in-Publication Data
Miller, Sara Swan.
  Better than TV / Sara Swan Miller ; illustrated by Michael Chesworth.
    p.   cm.
  "A Yearling first choice chapter book."
  Summary: When a power failure deprives them of television on a rainy day, two children and their dog entertain themselves and their family by creating and acting out their own television show.
ISBN 0-385-32325-5 (alk. paper).—ISBN 0-440-41355-9 (pbk. : alk. paper)
  [1. Television—Fiction.   2. Play—Fiction.   3. Dogs—Fiction.] I. Chesworth, Michael, ill.   II. Title.
PZ7. M63344Be   1998
[E]—dc20   96-34385
                                                               CIP
                                                               AC

Hardcover: The trademark Delacorte Press® is registered in the U.S. Patent and Trademark Office and in other countries.
Paperback: The trademark Yearling® is registered in the U.S. Patent and Trademark Office and in other countries.

The text of this book is set in 17-point Baskerville.
Book design by Ericka Meltzer
Manufactured in the United States of America
February 1998
10 9 8 7 6 5 4 3 2

BETTER THAN TV

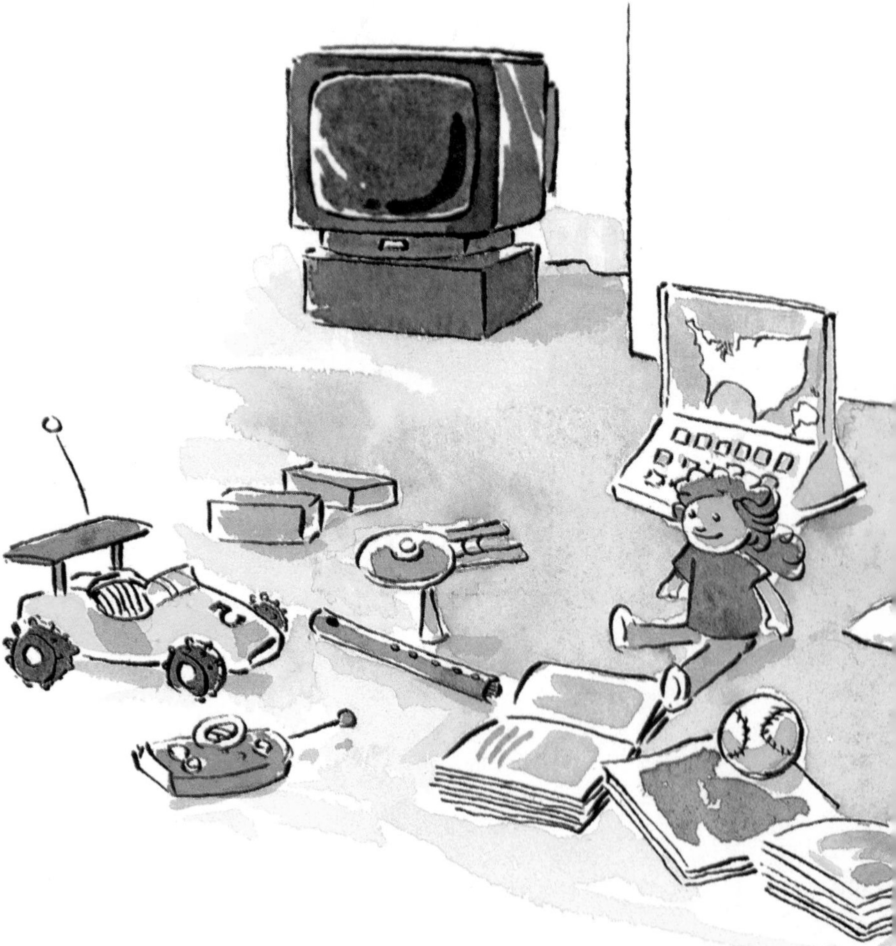

CONTENTS

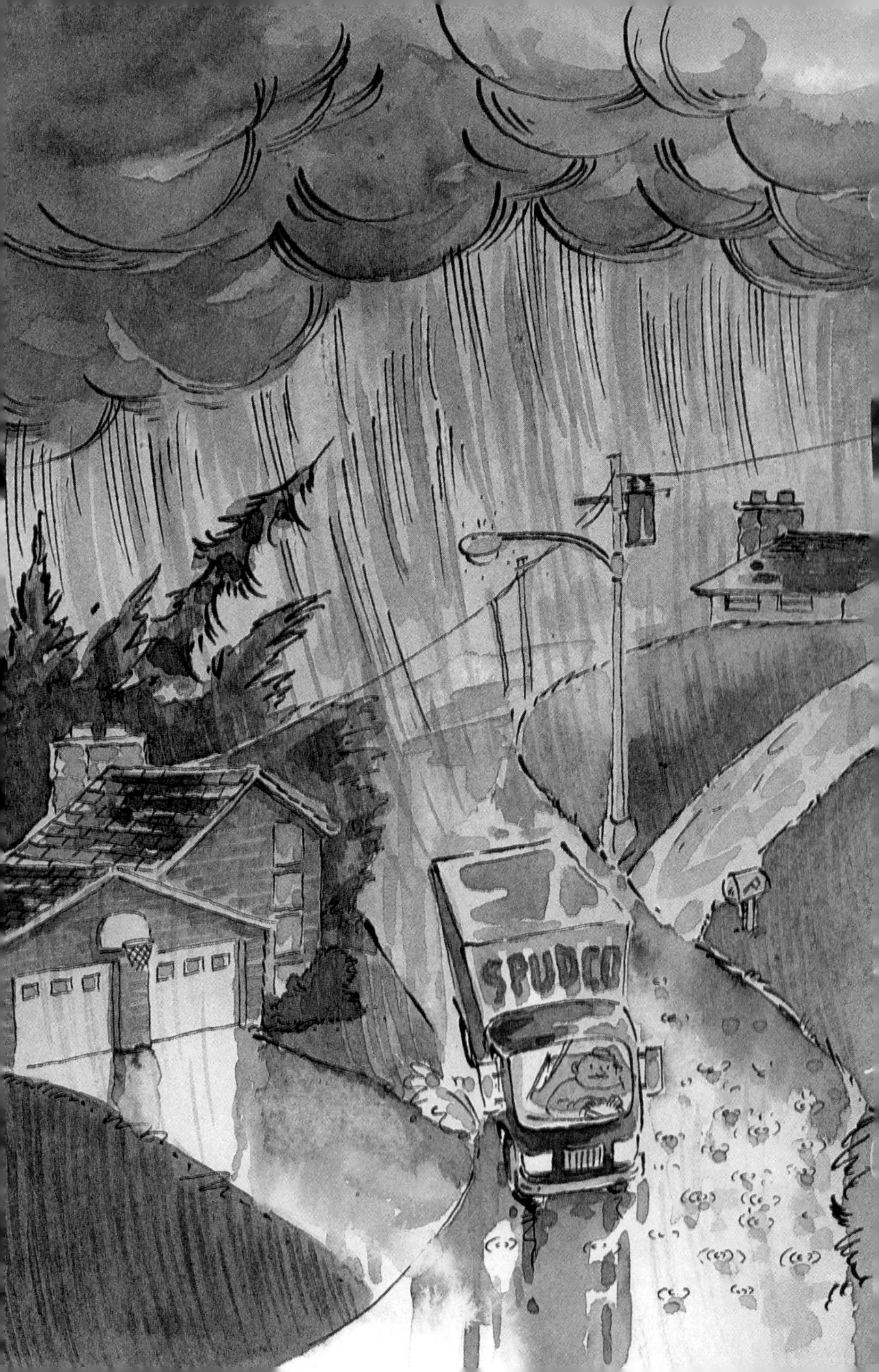
SPUDCO

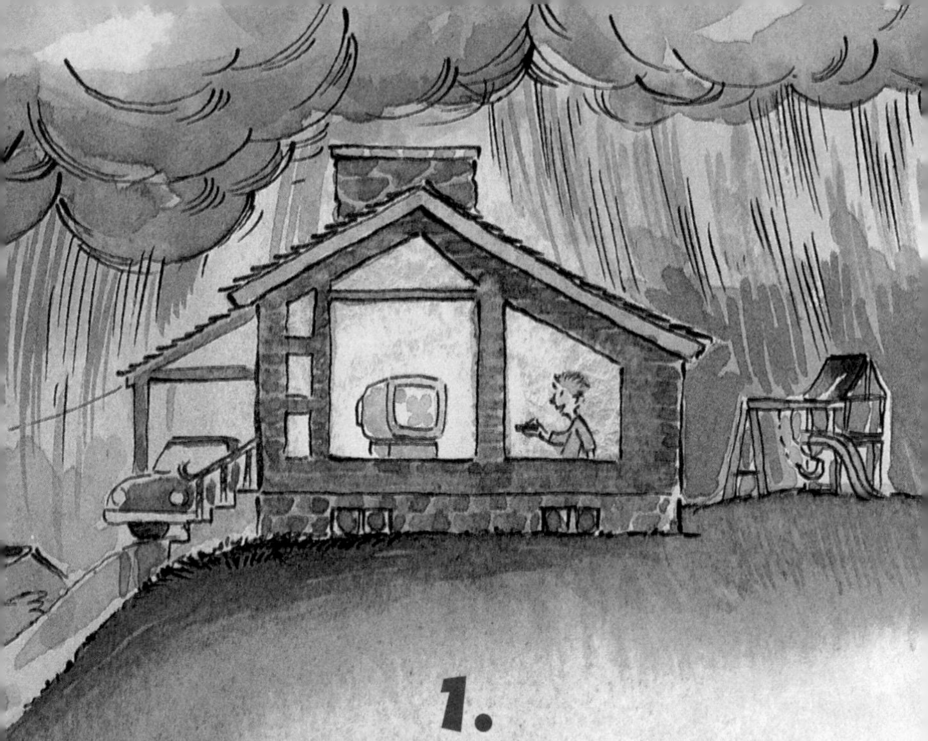

1.
A STORMY DAY

Rain was coming down
in buckets outside.
The wind was blowing
the trees inside out.
But Chris and Erin didn't care.
It was time for their favorite TV show.

"Bring the pretzels, Erin,"
called Chris.
"Only if you bring the gumdrops!"
yelled Erin.
Fred the dog sat between them
on the couch.
It was his favorite show too.
Chris hit the remote.

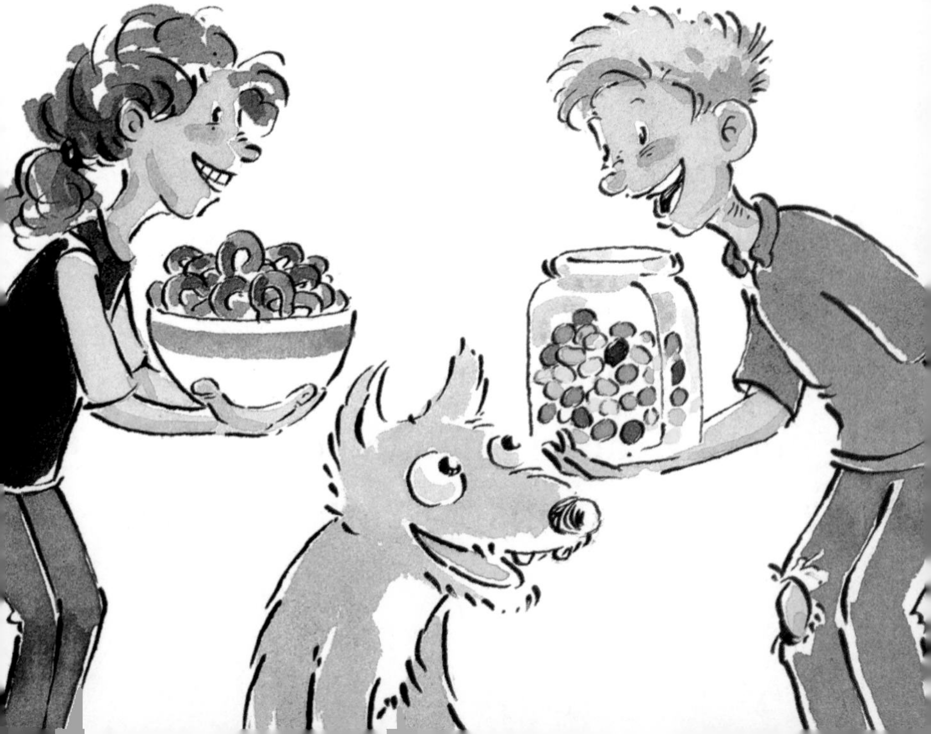

"And now . . . ," he said.

"Teenage Mooing Ninja Cows!"
sang the TV.

"Pass the pretzels," said Chris.

"Pass the gumdrops!" thought Fred.

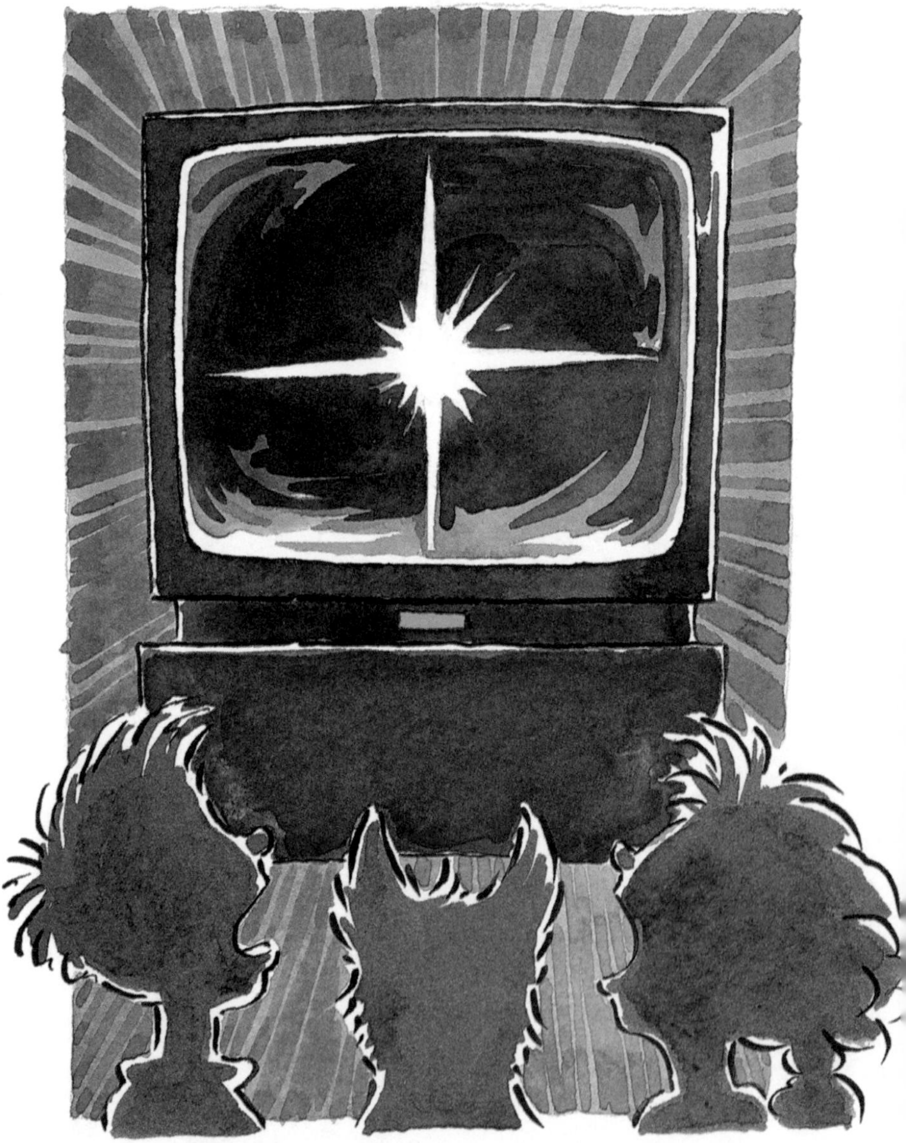

All at once the TV went *pop!*

The screen went black.

"Hey!" Chris and Erin yelled.

Erin pounded on the top of the TV.

Chris gave it a good kick.

Fred tried licking the screen.

Nothing happened.

"Mom!" shouted Erin.

"Mom!" shouted Chris.

"Take it easy," said Mom.

"It's not the end of the world.

And *don't* feed that dog gumdrops!"

"Hurry, Mom. Fix it!" cried Erin.

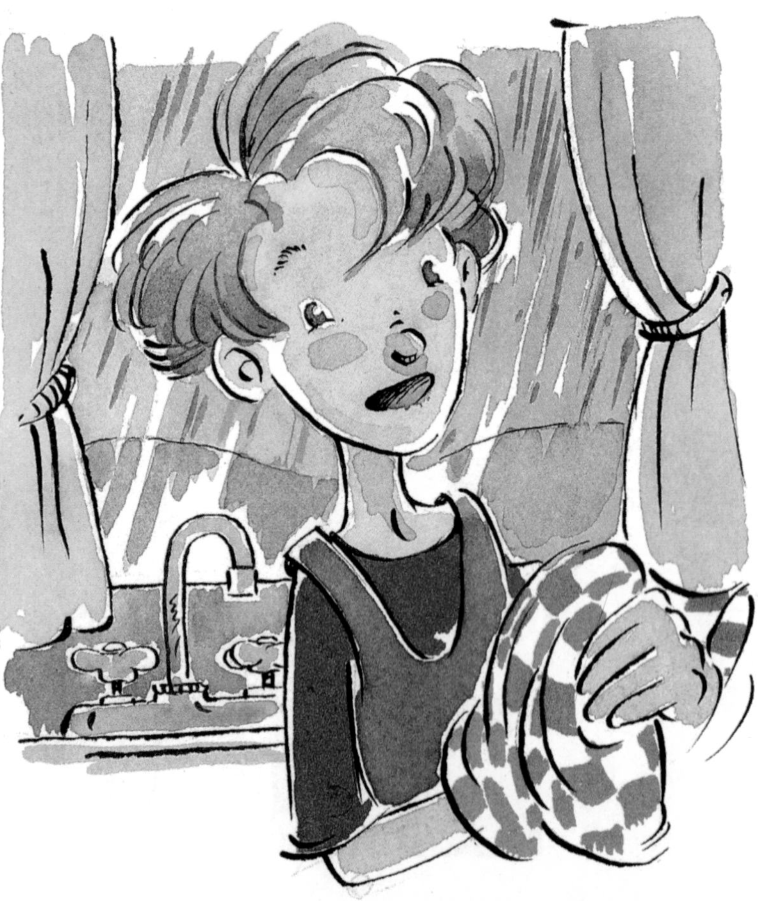

"It's not broken, dear."

They looked at the TV again.

"The lights are off too," said Mom.

"No power, no TV."

Chris kicked the TV again.

"Rats!" he yelled.

Erin gave it another good smack.

"Phooey!" she yelled.

Fred smeared nose juice on it.

"Rough!" he barked.

"What are we going to do now?"

moaned Chris and Erin.

"Why don't you go play outside?"
said Mom.
Erin and Chris and Fred
just looked at her.
Mom looked out the window.

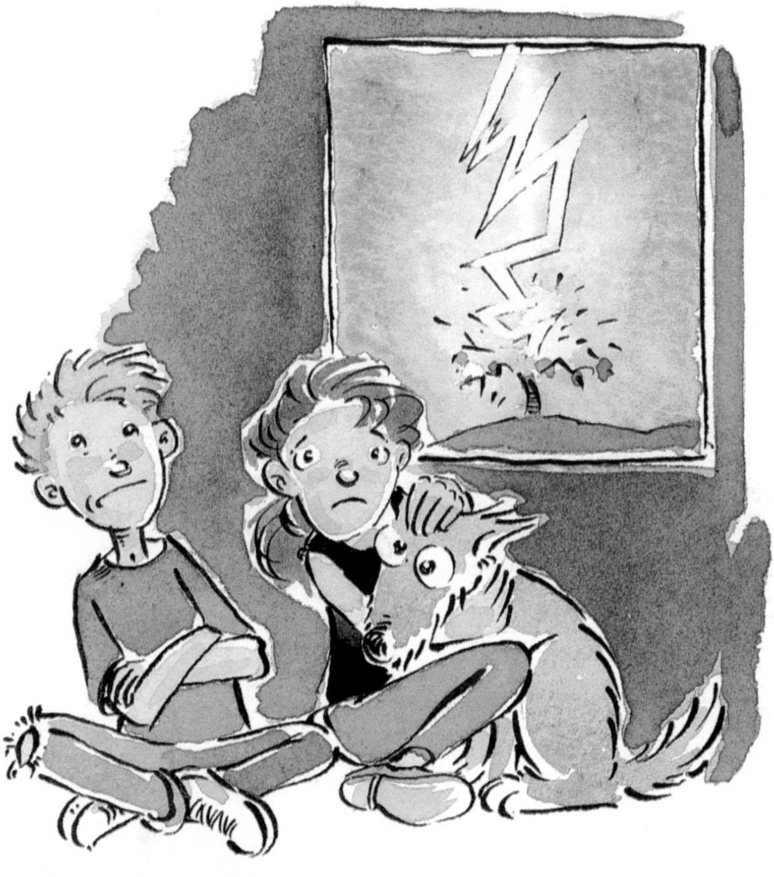

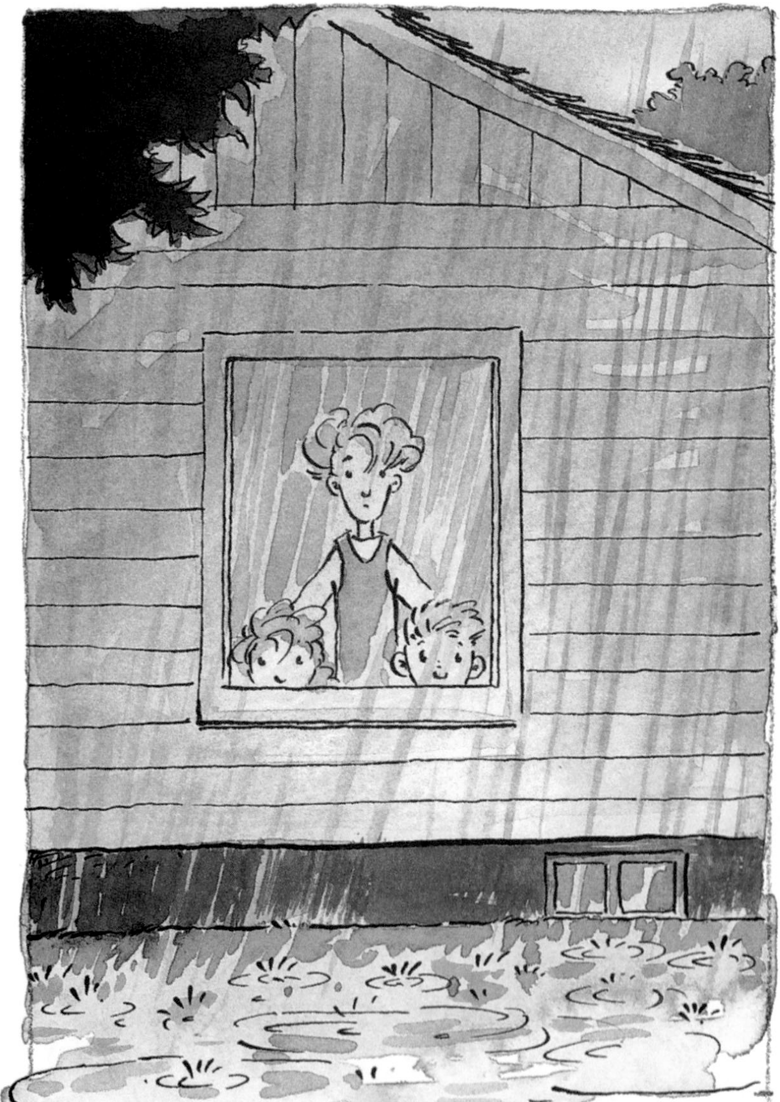

"Oops! Bad idea," she said.

Fred picked up his squeaky toy.

Squeaky! Squeaky! went Fred.

He wagged his tail.

"Why don't you play with Fred?"
said Mom.

"Good idea!" thought Fred.

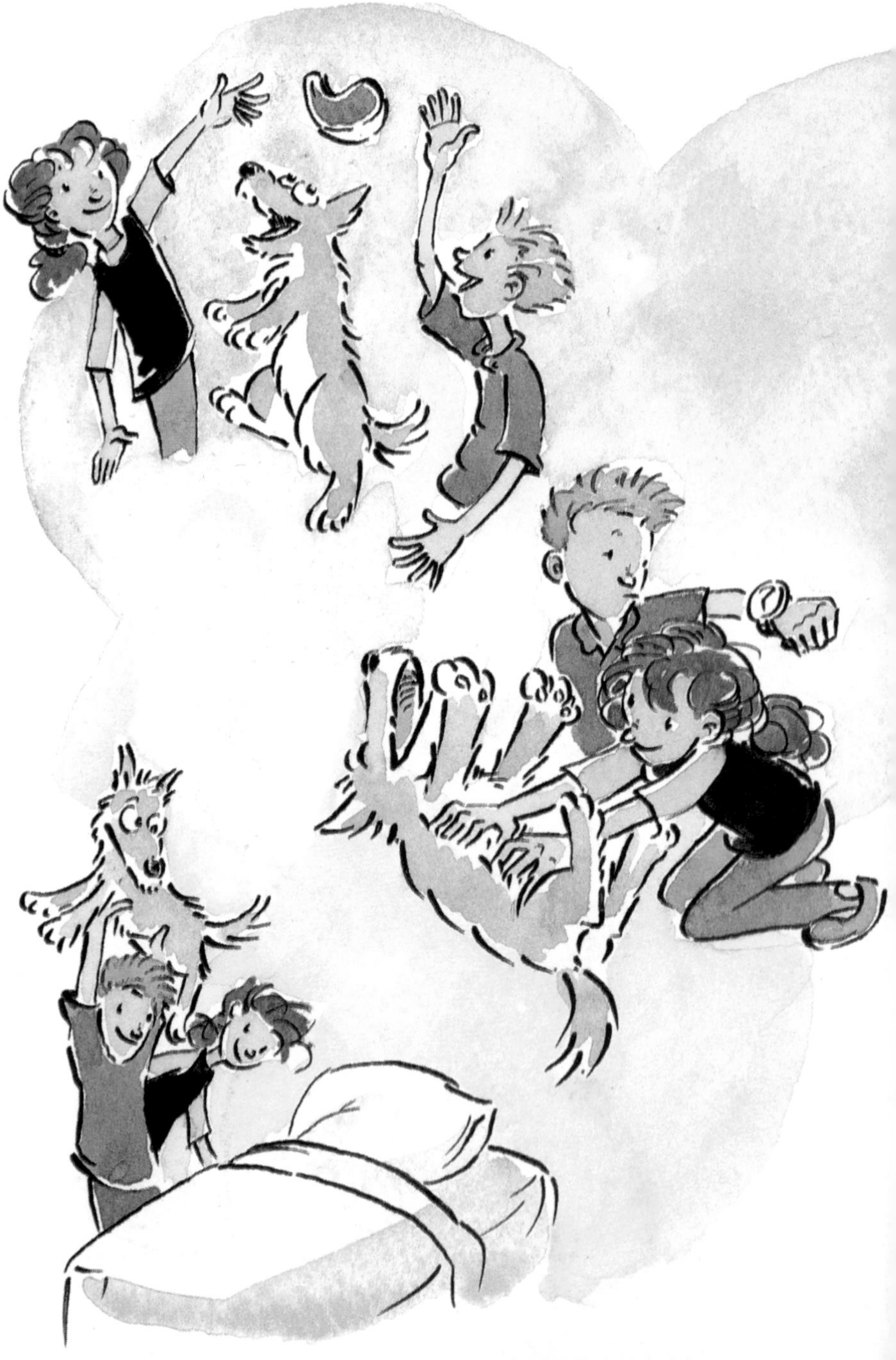

2.
FRED HELPS OUT

Chris and Erin played with Fred.

They played Fred-in-the-Middle.

They played Tickle Fred.

They played Bounce-Fred-on-the-Bed.

"Whew!" thought Fred. "I'm tired."

He crawled under the bed.

"So much for playing with Fred,"
said Erin.

"Now what are we going to do?"
said Chris.

"Why don't you go play outside?"
said Dad.

Chris and Erin just looked at him.

Dad looked out the window.

"Guess not," he said.

"How about drawing some pictures?"
he said.

Chris and Erin shrugged.

It was better than nothing.

Fred crawled out from under the bed.

He watched them work.

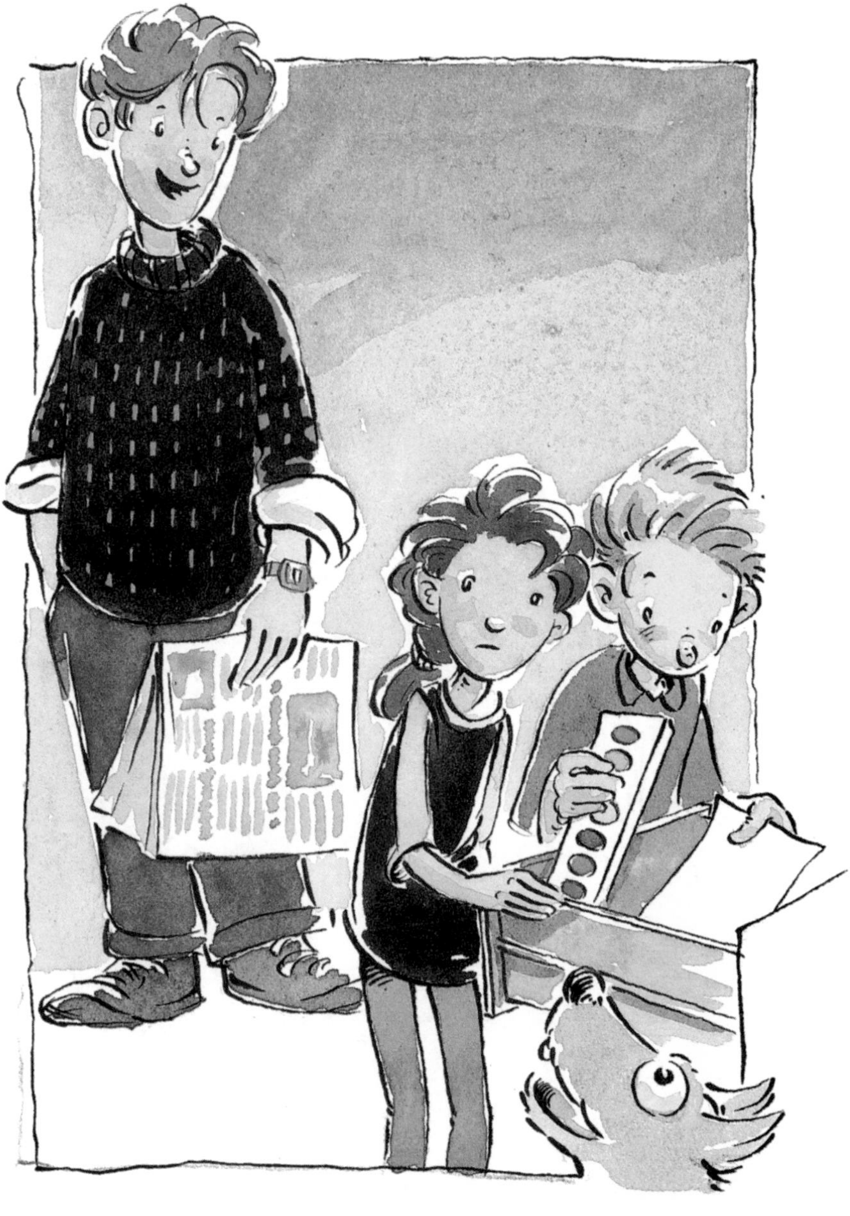

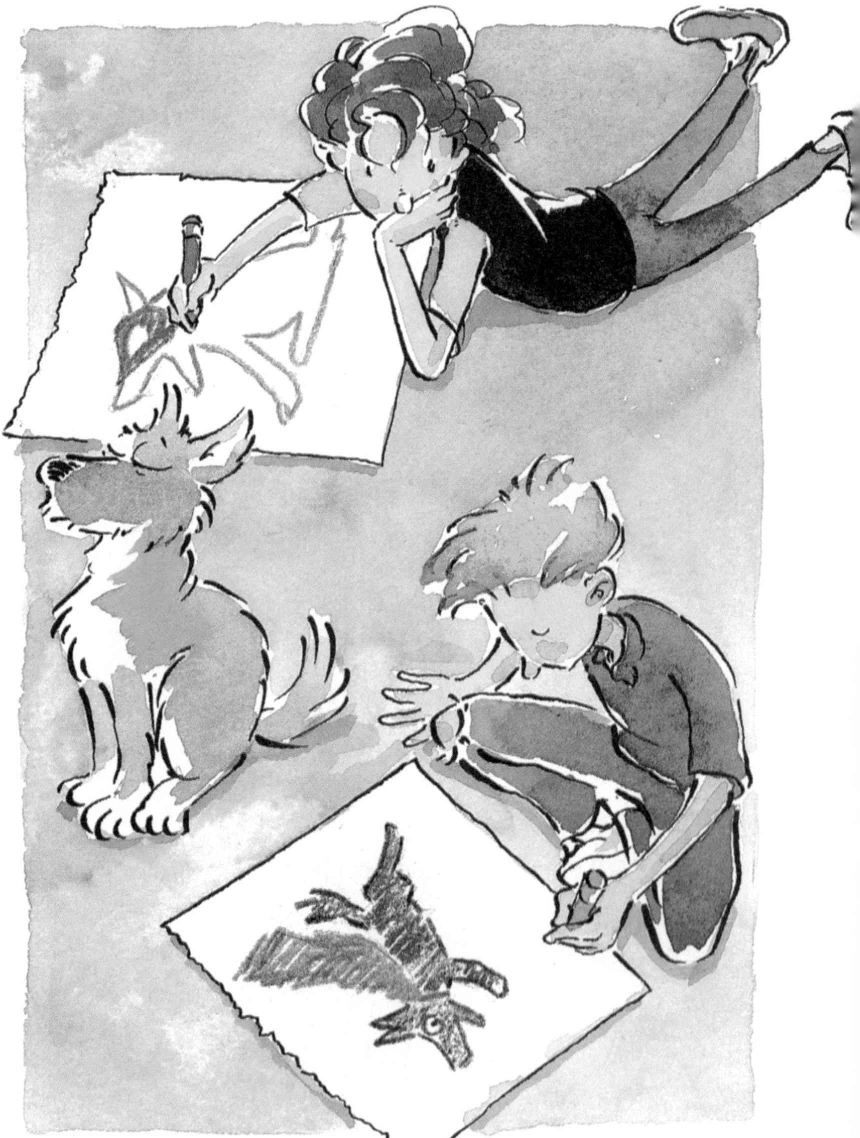

"What's that?" said Chris.

"Fred as a Teenage Drooling Ninja Pooch," said Erin. "What's yours?"

"Fred as Superdog," said Chris.
Fred thought he looked
very handsome.

He ate both pictures.

"*Fred!*" Chris and Erin yelled.

"Now what are we going to do?"

"Why don't you go play outside?"
said Grandma.

"Doesn't anyone ever look out
the window?" said Chris.

"Then why don't you build a house?"

"A house?" said Erin.

"But we're not carpenters!"

"With blocks," said Grandma.

Fred watched them build a house.

It took a long time.

Finally his doghouse was done.

He tried it out.

"*Fred!*" yelled Chris and Erin.

"Look what you did!"

Fred hid under the couch.

"Now what are we going to do?"
said Chris.

"I don't know," said Erin.

"I know!" said Grandpa.

"Don't tell us to go play outside,"
 said Chris.

"Of course not," said Grandpa.
"It's raining cats and dogs out there!"
Fred crawled out from
under the couch.
But he didn't see any cats
raining anywhere.
"Listen," said Grandpa.
"Here's my idea."

3.
A GOOD IDEA

"What's going on in the basement?"
asked Mom. "I hear a lot of giggling."

"I hear a lot of barking," said Dad.

"And what's all that banging?"
asked Grandma.

Grandpa didn't say anything.

At last Chris came upstairs.
“Time for the show,” he said.
“Come one, come all!”

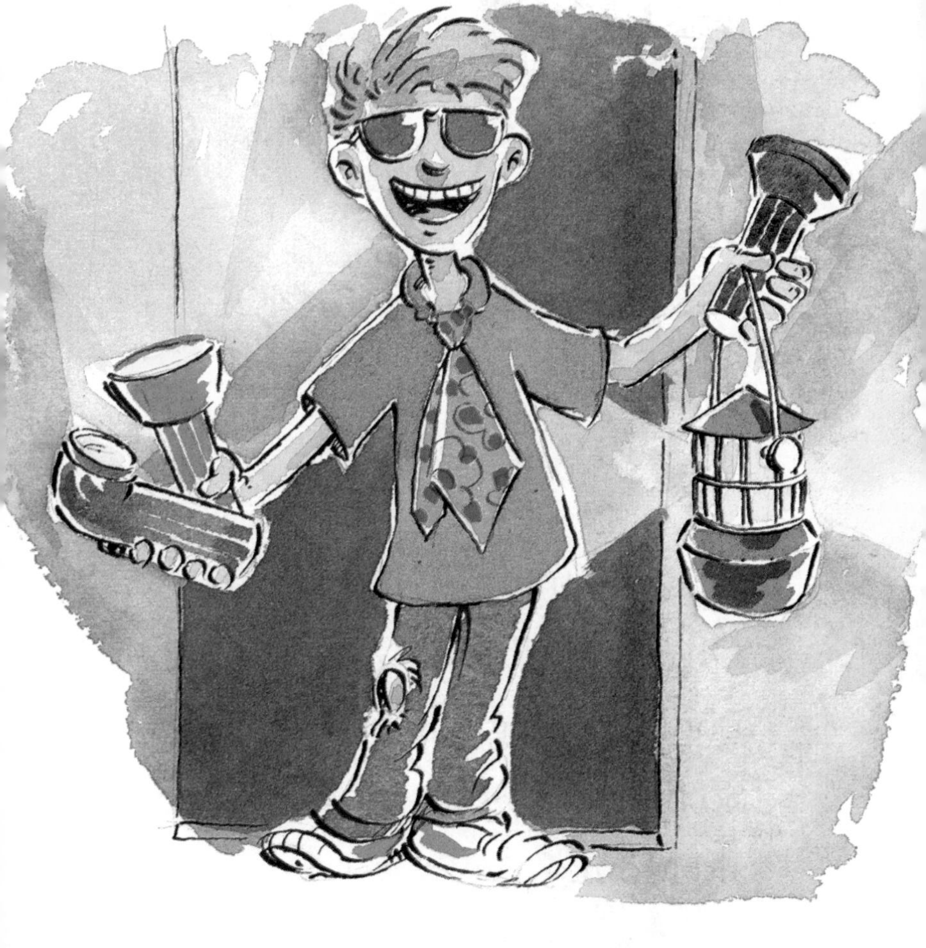

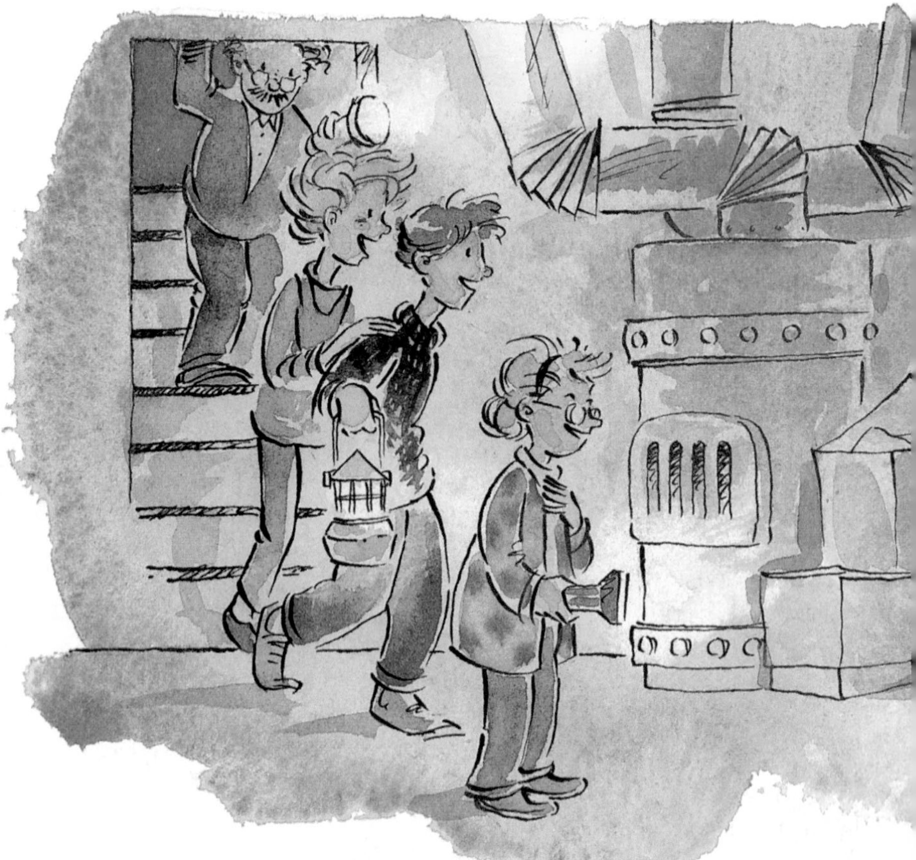

Everyone tramped downstairs.

"Oh, a stage!" said Grandma.

"Looks like a giant TV," said Dad.

"So that's why they took my sheet," said Mom.

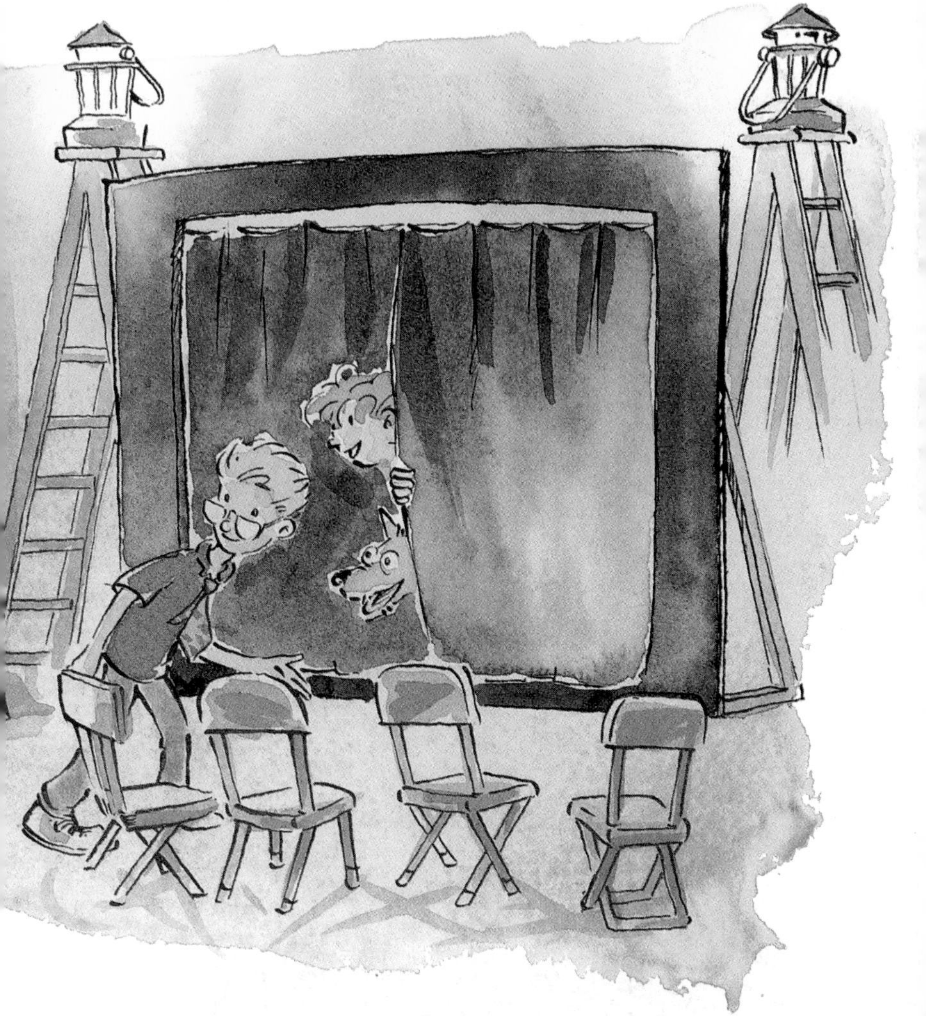

"And my ladders," said Dad.

Grandpa just smiled.

"Sit down, everyone," said Erin.

"Here, Dad," said Chris.

"You get the remote."

Chris and Erin and Fred ran

behind the sheet.

"Hit Channel Six!" called Chris.

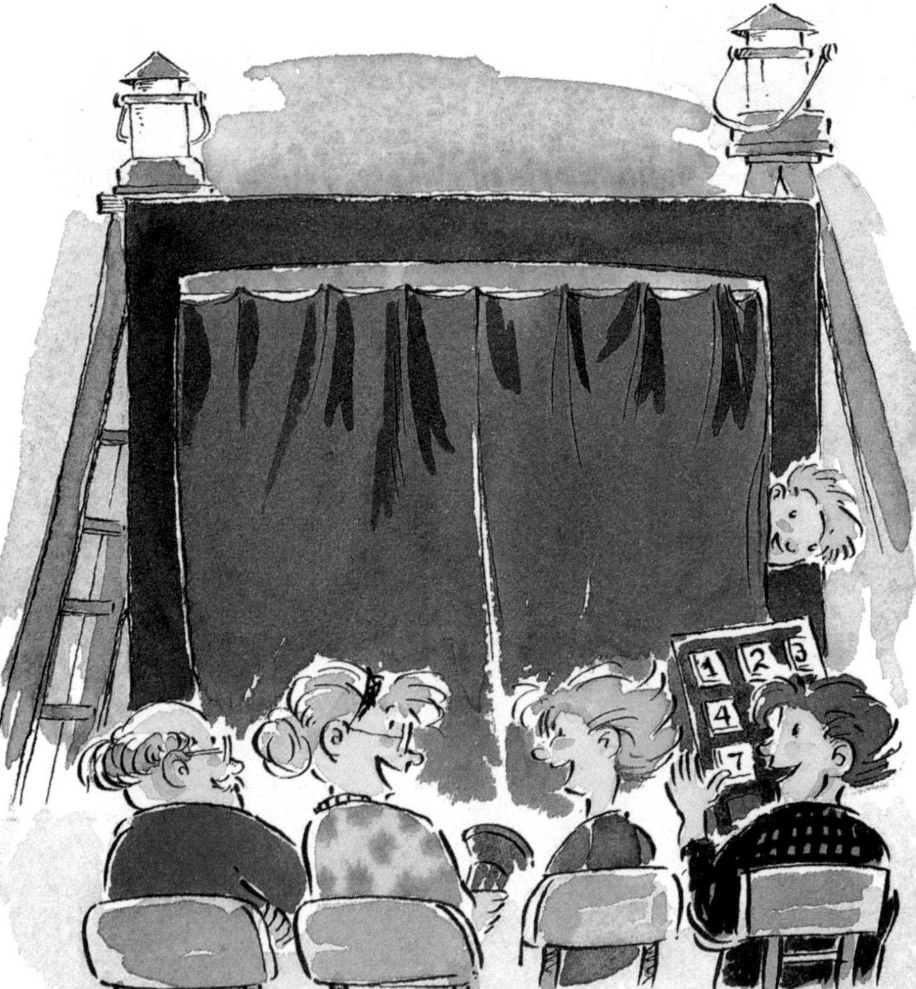
1 2 3
4
7

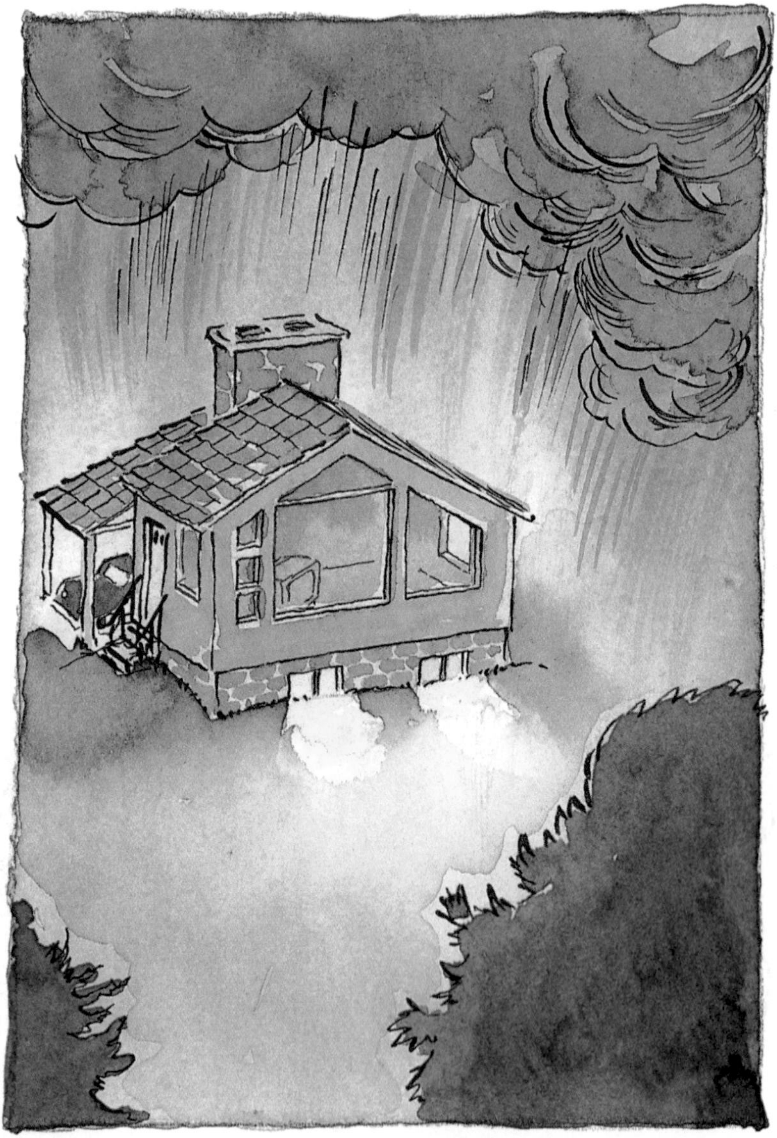

4.
CHANGE THE CHANNEL!

Dad hit Channel Six.

The curtain yanked open.

Chris wore a shaggy black wig.

Erin wore a shaggy blond wig.

Fred had on a green wig.

And he wore a ukulele

around his neck.

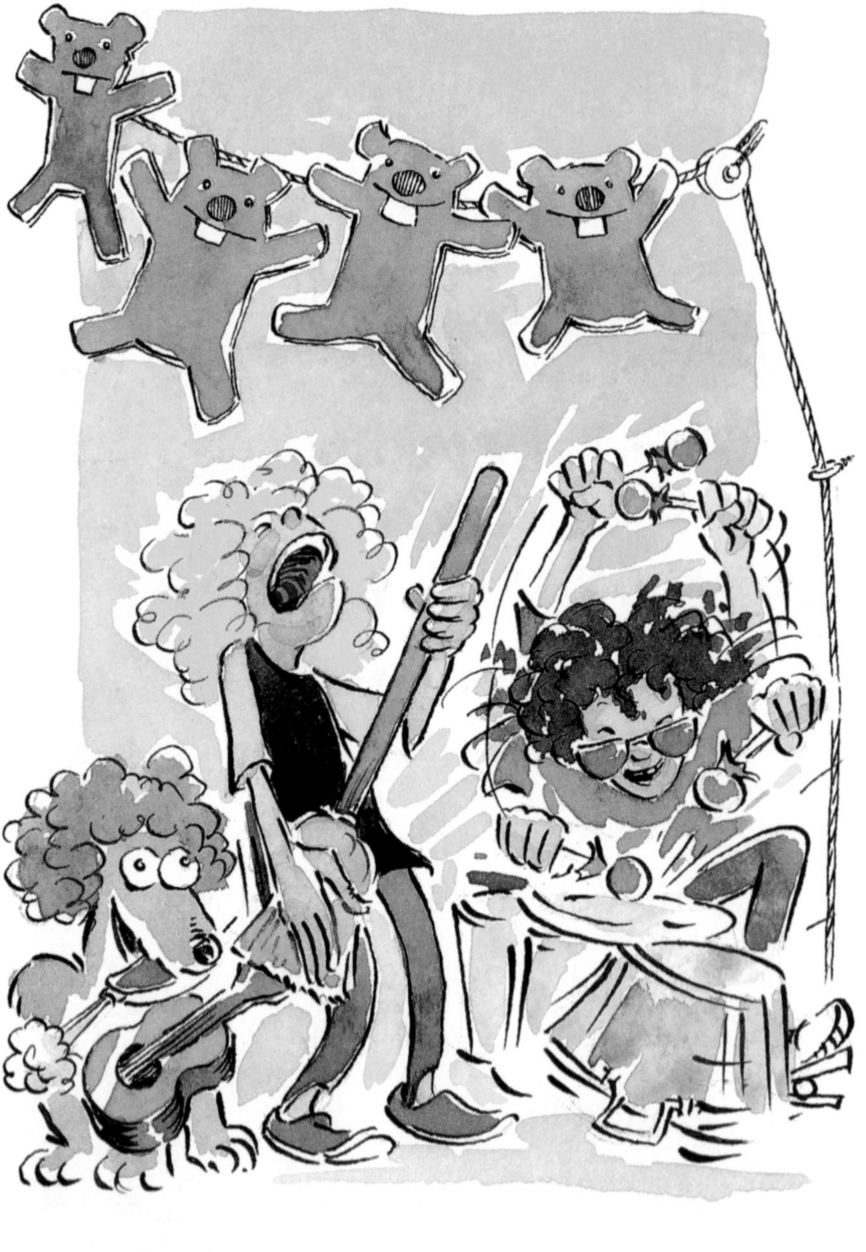

"Oh," said Mom, "a music video!"

Fred squeaked his squeaky toy.

Erin and Chris danced and sang:

"Great green gobs of

greasy grimy gopher guts.

Mutilated monkey meat.

Little dirty birdies' feet.

Great green gobs of

greasy grimy gopher guts.

And me without my spoon!"

"Yay!" called Dad.

"Wait," said Chris.

"There's more."

"Fate feen fobs of
feasy fimey fofer futs . . ."
They went through F.
Then they did S:
"Sate seen sobs of
seasy simey sofer suts . . ."
Then they did J.
Fred squeaked away on his
squeaky toy.
They started in on M.
"I think it's time to change the
channel," said Grandma.

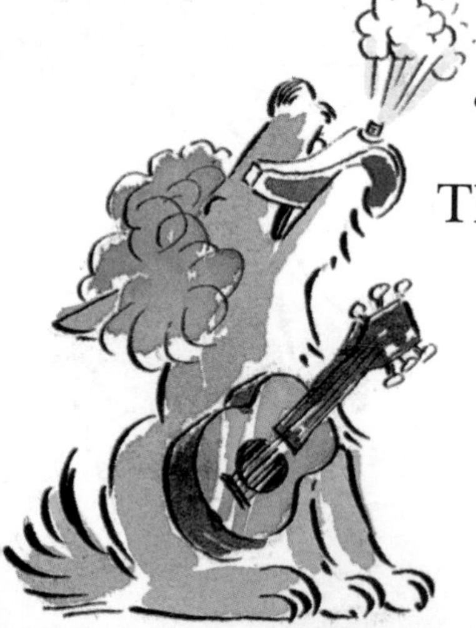

"Oh, okay," said Erin.
"Hit Off, Dad," said Chris.
The curtain yanked closed.

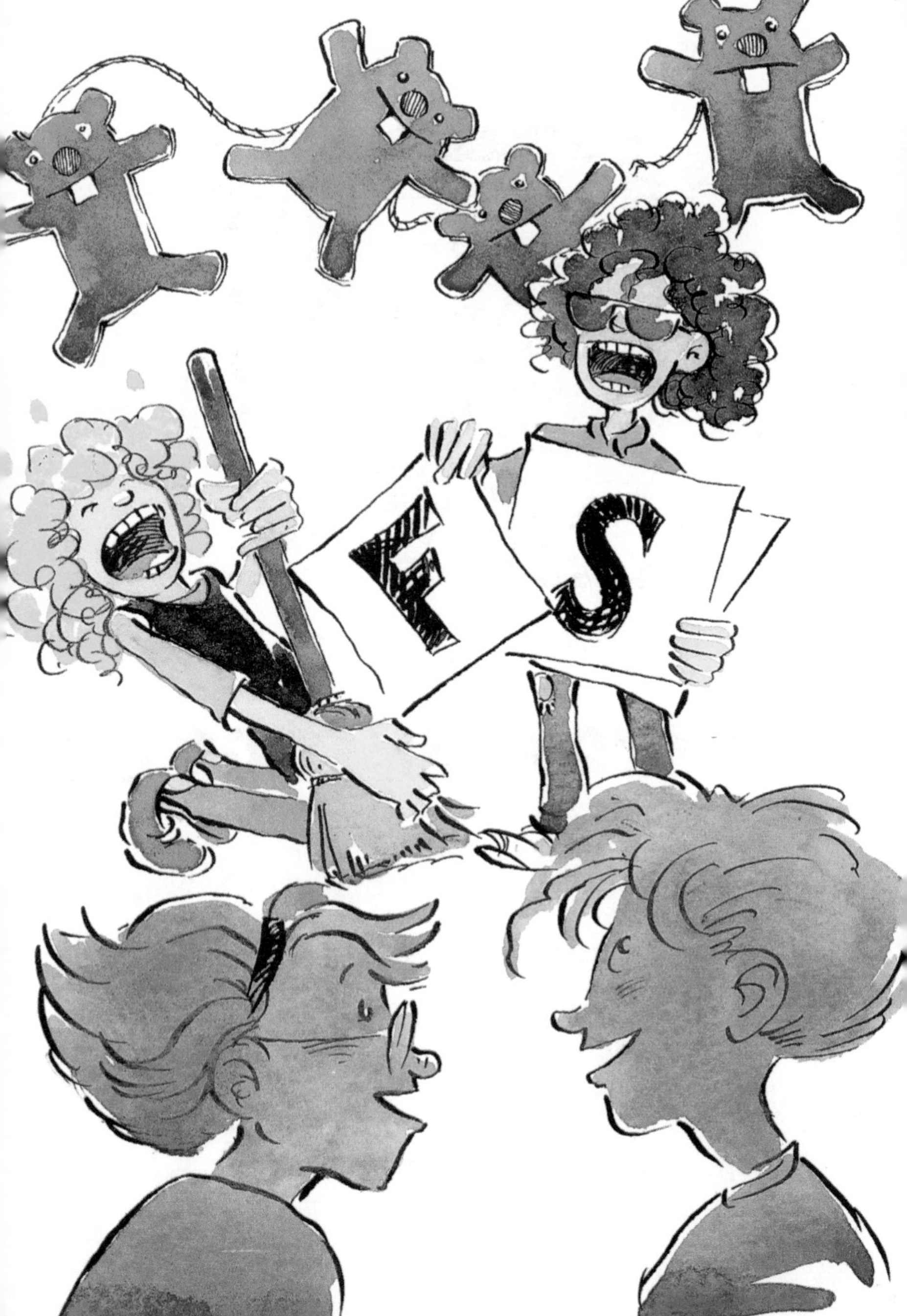
F
S

5.
THE SHOW MUST GO ON

Everyone waited.

Scrape shuffle scrape.

Shuffle scrape shuffle.

"Hit Channel Five!"
called Chris at last.

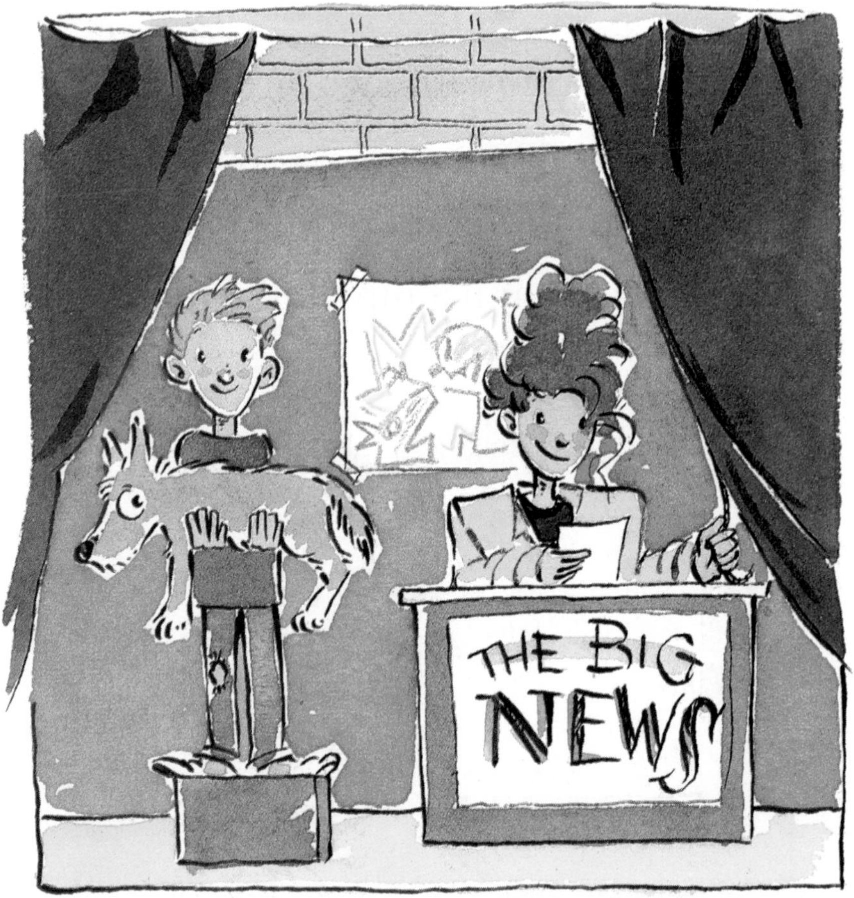
THE BIG
NEWS

Erin sat behind a desk.

Chris held on to Fred.

"And now, the news," said Erin.

"The top story today:
Boy bites dog!"
"Uh-oh," thought Fred.
Chris gave him a nip on the neck.

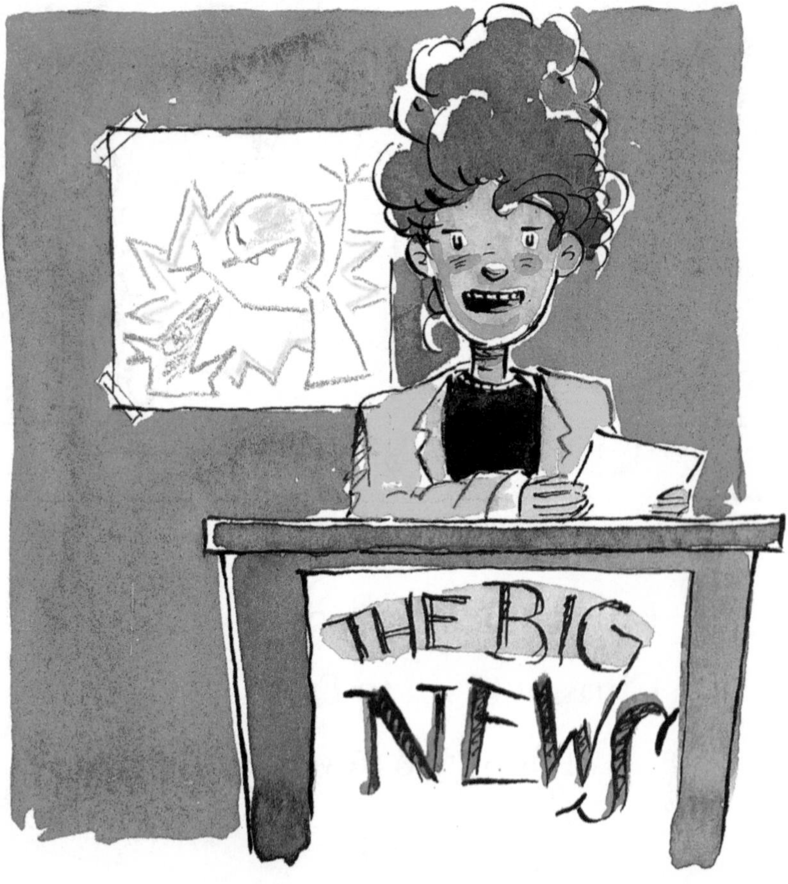
THE BIG
NEWS

"Tell us, Chris," said Erin Newsgirl.

"How did that taste?

Speak right into the . . .

um . . . spoon."

"Yuck," said Chris. "Like dandruff!"

"Serves you right," thought Fred.

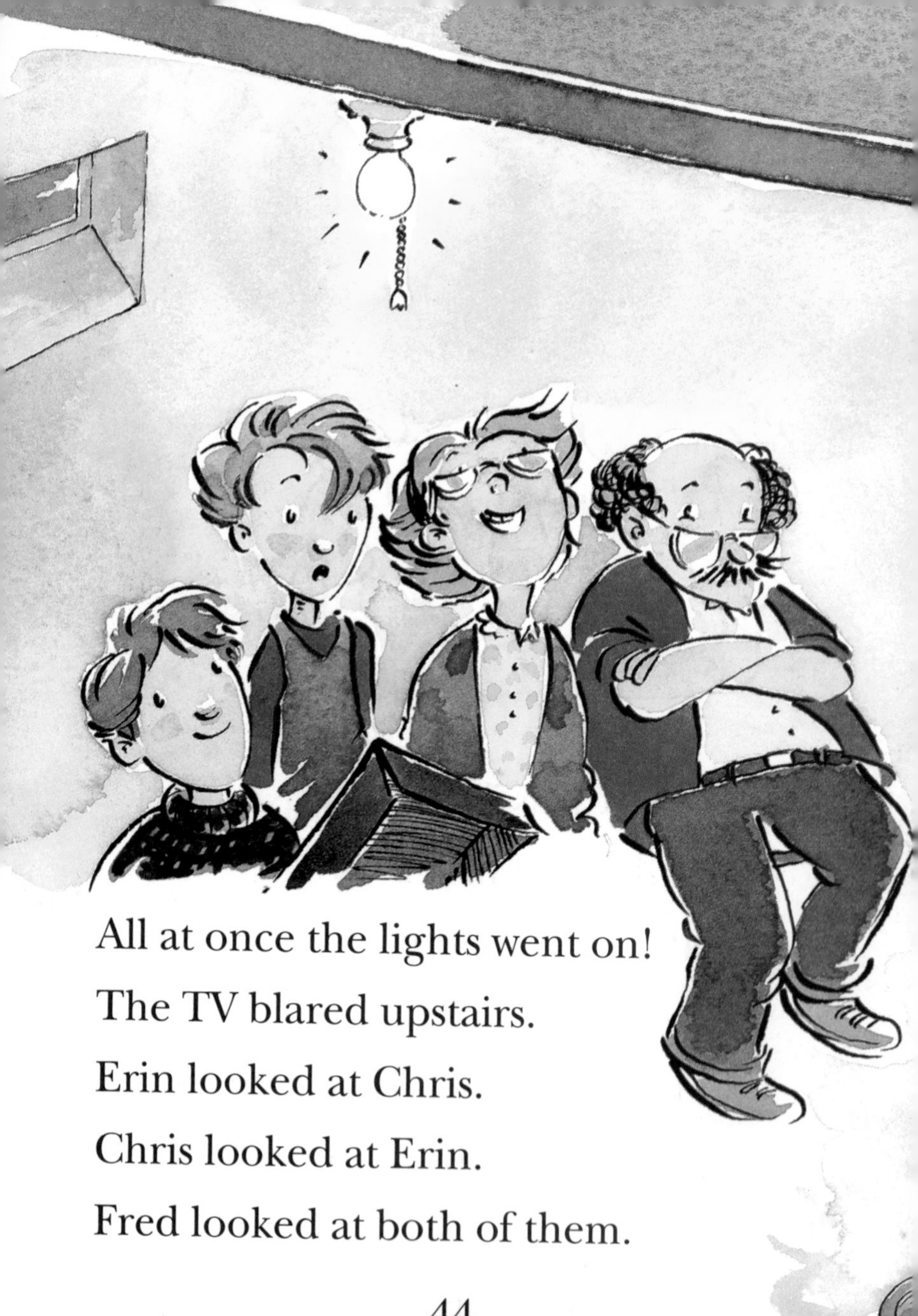

All at once the lights went on!
The TV blared upstairs.
Erin looked at Chris.
Chris looked at Erin.
Fred looked at both of them.

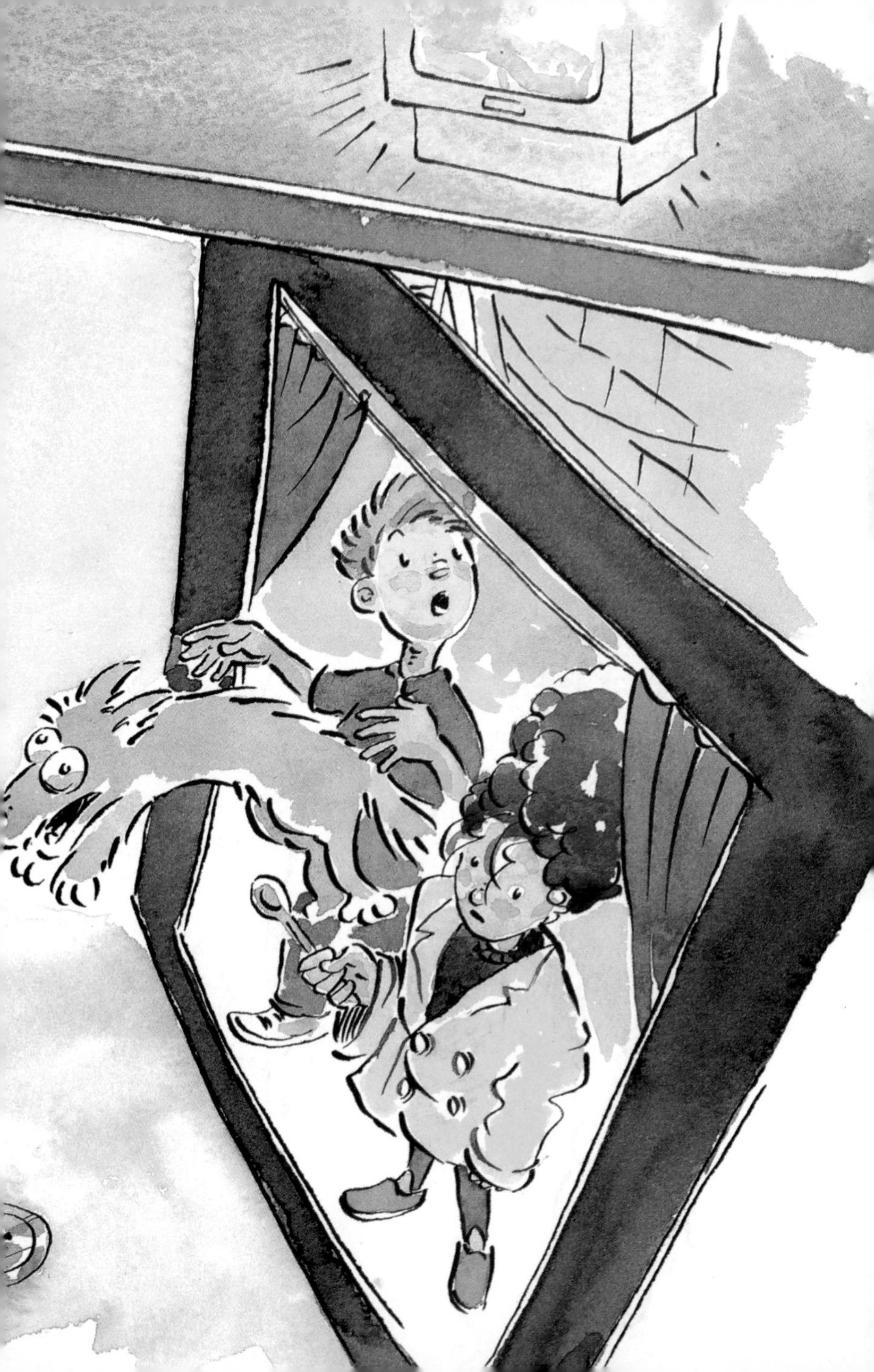

"Who cares?" said Chris.

"This is more fun," said Erin.

"And next in the news,
dentists say gumdrops are good
for your teeth.

Even dogs' teeth!"

"Here, Fred," called Chris.

"Next channel!" called Mom.

"Pass the pretzels," said Grandpa.

Fred just wagged his tail.

About the Author

Sara Swan Miller has written a number of stories for children's magazines and is the author of several children's books, including *Three Stories You Can Read to Your Dog*. She lives in New York.

About the Illustrator

Michael Chesworth has illustrated many picture books, including *Archibald Frisby*, which he wrote. He is also the illustrator of Judy Delton's Harry stories in *Spider* magazine. He lives in Connecticut.